The Adventures of No Feet Miller

Rocky Mtn. Ministries
Presents

The Adventures of No Feet Miller

Based on a true story

ReadersMagnet, LLC

The Adventures of No Feet Miller
Copyright © 2022 by Phyllis Glissan. All rights reserved.

Published in the United States of America
ISBN Paperback: 978-1-955603-16-4
ISBN eBook: 978-1-955603-15-7

All rights reserved. No part of this publication may be reproduced, stored in a retrieval system or transmitted in any way by any means, electronic, mechanical, photocopy, recording or otherwise without the prior permission of the author except as provided by USA copyright law.

The opinions expressed by the author are not necessarily those of ReadersMagnet, LLC.

ReadersMagnet, LLC
10620 Treena Street, Suite 230 | San Diego, California, 92131 USA
1. 619. 354. 2643 | www.readersmagnet.com

Book design copyright © 2022 by ReadersMagnet, LLC. All rights reserved.
Cover design by Kent Gabutin
Interior design by Renalie Malinao

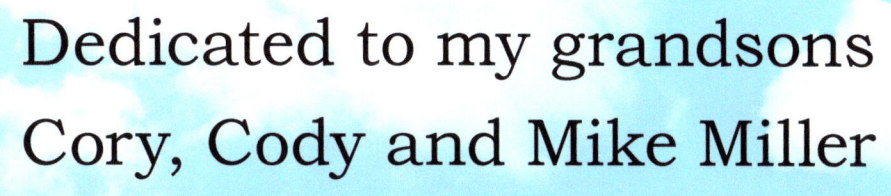

Dedicated to my grandsons
Cory, Cody and Mike Miller

Meet Miller

Hi there, my friends call me "Miller".

I am here to tell you a great story. My friends still talk about those amazing days a long time ago. When I went on an adventure all alone.

The Dream.

I was young and free. I set out on a journey to see what I could see, to be all I could be.

Leaving my home.

Deep in the foothills is Rocky Mountain Acres, my home. My family and friends came together that day to wish me well. Sending me on my way.

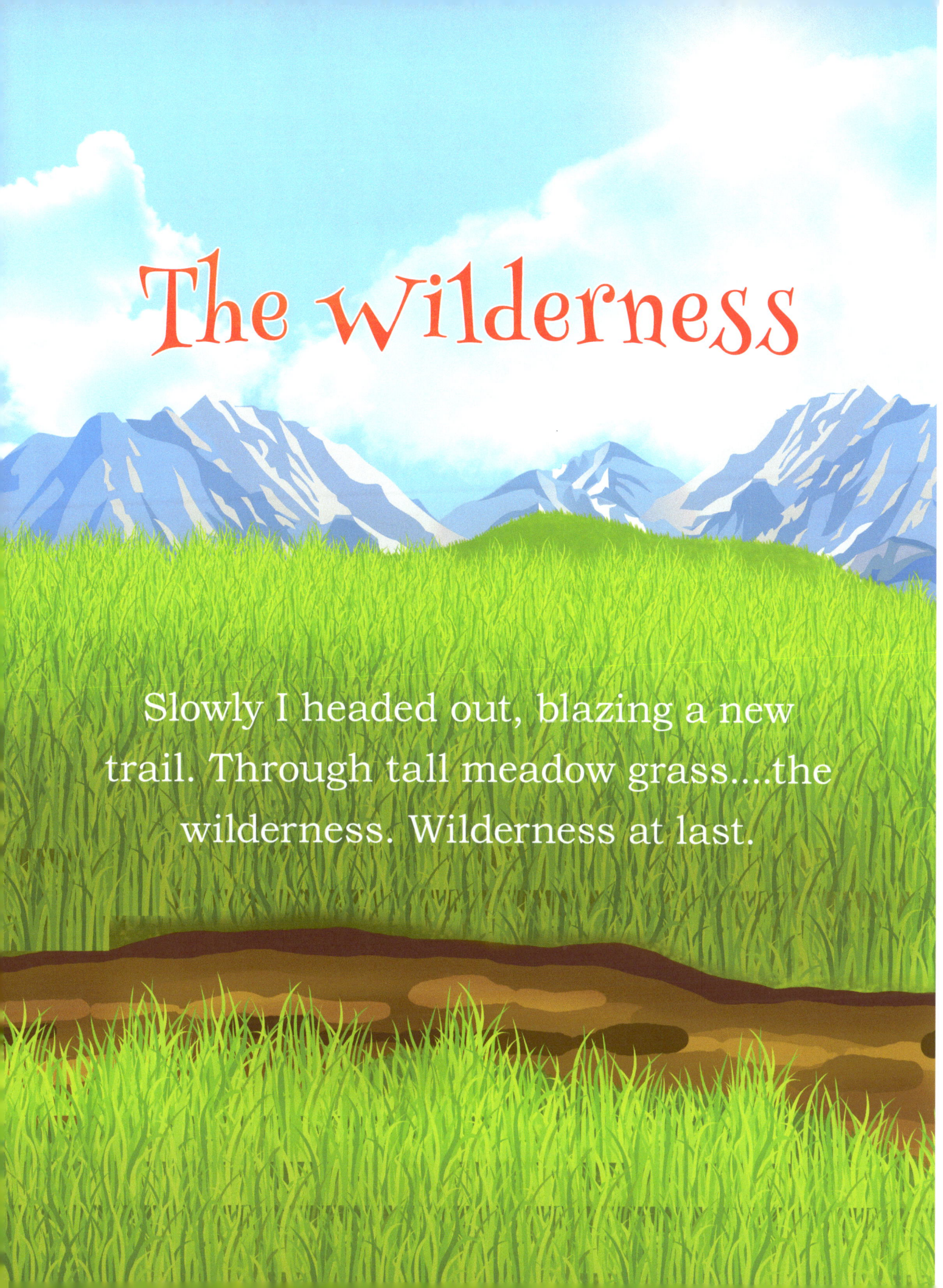

The Wilderness

Slowly I headed out, blazing a new trail. Through tall meadow grass....the wilderness. Wilderness at last.

All Alone Now

All alone now. What do you know about things? Your family I will pray. This part of very special, looking at all of God's creations. The living creatures in the wilderness, my oh my.

God's Creatures

Speaking of creatures, I have a confession to make. In the bible, Genesis 1, when God was creating the earth; verse 24 tells about when God made creeping things. Yep, that's me. Some call me No Feet Miller. A trusting, charming, adventurist snake.

3rd Day Exploring

I traveled all day, eating wild fruits as I went. But, now the sun sets in the western sky. Oh my, quickly I must find a hollow tree log to give me warmth and safety.

A Night of Terror

I had been asleep for hours. Suddenly I became restless and awake. What is this? I could hear a screeching, terrifying sound in the distance. The ground under me seems to be shivering and that indescribable noise is coming closer. Getting louder and louder.

To Be Brave

What ever will I do? This noise is hurting my ears, and the ground is rumbling. One thing I know for sure is that what ever is , it is not from God. I took courage and slowly stretched long scared body to the opening of the log. Being ever so careful, I peered out.

My Friends Warned Me

I take one quick glance over my right shoulder. Will I escape in time? My friends did warn me there would be days like this. My buddy Duke, a llama, said; "Never travel alone". Pepper, the mini donkey, final words to me were, "Never, I say never, cross a road". Sweet Suzette, the pygmy goat, warned me; "Miller, beware of train tracks". Sooner or later a huge screeching at that very moment my thoughts were silent.

In Harms Way

Go Miller Go!

Twisting and turning, fast as I can go. BOY, could I use a pair of running feet right now! Oh Oh! finally I am free of the log. But I don't feel safe yet. You, yes you, can help me. Say this with me; Go Miller Go!

The Narrow Escape

Dear God in heaven, this is it. The train tracks, and that is a train. Exactly the way Suzette described to me. Go Miller go is all I can do now. If I could only make it to that tree my life will be saved. The noise and the beaming light seemed to be everywhere, I mean everywhere! But I will not give up! I can do this! I closed my eyes and made one very desperate leap to safety. A very close call.

Safe At Last

Flying swiftly through the air, I hit that tree with a loud splat. Quick as a flash, I wrapped myself around the tree trunk and I was safe. Minutes later the train had passed, but I was to scared to move. A half hour had gone by and I began to slowly lower my body to the ground.

A New Beginning

A brand new day of tall grass and trees. The following three days were all the same. I must tell you, traveling is an adventure, but being alone is not fun. It can fearful and is a time to be aware of your safety. Even the wild animals travel together, seeking food and safety. The good thing is, God is watching over you. I am beginning to believe in the words Duke said to me, "Never travel alone".

The Journey Home

The good news is I'm heading for home. God said all things have a season, meaning all things happen at a certain time. Like growing up and attending school, or going on an adventure. My adventure is soon to end. In a few days I will be home. My friends, my dear friends. I miss them so.

The End

10620 Treena Street, Suite 230
San Diego, California,
CA 92131 USA
www.readersmagnet.com
1.619.354.2643
Copyright 2022 All
Rights Reserved

www.ingramcontent.com/pod-product-compliance
Lightning Source LLC
LaVergne TN
LVHW070451080526
838202LV00035B/2803